Feast of Fools!

by

Jim Landis

DORRANCE PUBLISHING CO
EST. 1920
PITTSBURGH, PENNSYLVANIA 15238

Dorrance Publishing Co
585 Alpha Drive
Suite 103
Pittsburgh, PA 15238
Visit our website at *www.dorrancebookstore.com*

ISBN: 979-8-88812-364-5
eISBN: 979-8-88812-864-0

FEAST OF FOOLS!
A PLAY IN TWO ACTS

CAST LIST
In Order of Appearance

JOHN ANDERSON, 50's, is a typical Midwest father. Handsome in a weekend golfer kind of way.

MARIE ANDERSON, 50's, she is a nice-looking woman, but years of smoking and drinking alcohol have started to show.

SEAN ANDERSON, 20's, a muscular all-American college kid.

CHET, 30's, preppy and perfectly dressed in Ralph Lauren. He is a doctor and stuck in a different era.

LESLIE, late 20's, a kind hearted natural beauty.

UNCLE SONNY, mid-40's, gay and a bit soft around the edges. He has a warm smile and a kind soul.

LAVELLE, 40's, is a tall, effeminate African American man. He is a big presence.

AUNT BONNIE, 80's, a frail little shadow of a woman. Her crooked body moves like a marionette on her walker and her voice cuts through you like a knife.

JAPANESE NURSE, 40's, a small, stern, no nonsense caretaker.

HARVEST THEATER COMPANY

PRESENTS
The Original Production of

FEAST OF FOOLS!
A PLAY IN TWO ACTS
BY
JIM LANDIS

DIRECTED BY
TAMARA RUPPART

ORIGINAL CAST MEMBERS

MARIE ANDERSON	*Cathy McAuley*
JOHN ANDERSON	*Larry Poindexter*
SEAN	*J.T. Garcia*
LESLIE	*Katie Peabody*
CHET	*Peter Mitchell*
UNCLE SONNY	*Patrick Richwood*
LAVELLE	*Mark Nordike*
AUNT BONNIE	*Livia Trevino*
JAPANESE NURSE	*June Angela*

SOUND and VIDEO DESIGN
Bill Pomeroy

PROPERTIES
Rebecca Carranza

GRAPHIC DESIGN
Nina Howard

*This Production of 'Feast of Fools!' was originally performed in September of 2022 at the **GARRY MARSHALL THEATER** in Toluca Lake California.

George Winston's "Living In The Country" *begins to play.*

CURTAIN UP:

In the center, stands a projector screen. It's white reflection is a stark contrast against the BLACK stage. After a beat, a SLIDE of a beautiful mid-western home 'clicks' on.

SEAN (V.O.) I grew up in this house. I don't know a lot of people these days who can boast that. An entire childhood spent at 236 Martha Anne. Someone said, I was lucky. I still don't know why.

Another SLIDE of a closer shot of the home, clicks on. It shows an idyllic resident. Complete with wood siding and river rock accents.

SEAN (V.O.) Those top two windows, were my room. I made a lot of discoveries about myself in that space. I decided to be a firefighter, go to U.C. Berkley, recycle... (beat) I was confused a lot there too.

Another SLIDE showing a big backyard, clicks on.

SEAN (V.O.) We had a big backyard with a putting green for Dad and a garden for Mom, and there used to be cornfields everywhere! I only get home twice a year since I moved away to college, Christmas and Thanksgiving.

A SLIDE showing the house decorated as a winter wonderland, clicks on.

SEAN (V.O.) Ahhh, the holidays. My parents live for the holidays! All the decorating and weeks of preparation. My father, to this day, still drags out this nasty matte haired, old, electric department store Santa, and props it proudly on the porch.

A SLIDE of the matte haired Santa, clicks on. His arm is outstretched to the sky.

SEAN (V.O.) Only one arm works, and when it moves up and down it looks like he's saluting Hitler!

A SLIDE showing a dining room table set with a beautiful Thanksgiving feast, clicks on.

SEAN (V.O.) Thanksgiving again in the Anderson household. You know the day. The usual unusual crowd of widowed half cousins, sad singles and people you see once a year.

(beat) This year will be different though. Let's see, not too many of us this Thanks Day. My Great Aunt Bonnie from Boca Raton. My Uncle Sonny and his husband LaVelle, my sister Leslie and her husband Chet. And of course, I'm always encouraged to bring a 'friend.' Which translates into someone I'm dating.

A SLIDE showing a group shot of everyone smiling as they raise a glass, clicks on.

It is <u>UPSIDE</u> down!

SEAN (V.O.) Nevertheless, we'll all be there. Carrying our monkey's on our backs and lying to one another that life is grand, while our mouths are full of turkey!

The MUSIC ends.

The lights FADE UP to reveal the projector screen sitting in the middle of a living room. It is a modest two-story home that is decorated every inch for Fall.

A dining room / den area with a large table. A bar leading into the kitchen divided by shutters sits adjacent. The furniture is dated but well cared for. A couch, coffee table and chair, sit in front of a large TV that faces away from the audience.

JOHN ANDERSON *50s, the Father, fiddles with a slide projector.*

JOHN I can't stand it when these darn carousels get all mixed up. Marie, have you been touching my slides?

MARIE (O.S.) What?

JOHN (louder) Did you touch my slides?

MARIE (O.S.) Now why would I touch your damn slides?

JOHN Never mind. What are you doing?

MARIE (O.S.) I'm basting the turkey.

JOHN Again? Careful, you don't want to drown that bird.

MARIE ANDERSON, *50s, enters with an old wooden box of silverware. She is a nice looking woman, but years of smoking and drinking alcohol have started to take their toll.*

MARIE Are you still fooling with that damn slide projector?

She sets the box on the dining room table that is open for a leaf, then lights a cigarette.

MARIE Nobody likes slides anymore! It's an antiquated form of entertainment!

JOHN Sure they do. The kids always got a kick out of them.

MARIE If you say so.

JOHN What's better than sitting down after a big dinner than taking in a little slide show down memory lane?

MARIE Going into the bathroom and sticking a wooden spoon down my throat to make room for dessert!

JOHN That's not pretty, Marie.

MARIE I promised to love you John, that's all.

She examines the silver, as John takes down the slide screen.

MARIE I need the leaf to this table, and would you bring me a glass of whatever's open in the fridge. I think I opened that foul Dago Chardonnay Aunt Bonnie brought us last Christmas. Look behind Sean's soy milk.

John exits into the kitchen.

MARIE I swear to God, everyone in this family drinks a different kind of milk. When I was a girl milk was milk! My daughter and her Acidophilus, your Aunt Bonnie and her butter milk, and your brother Sonny, well we all know what kind of milk he likes!

She makes a 'Gay' hand gesture as John enters from the kitchen with a leaf for the dining table.

JOHN (he puts in the leaf) Don't make fun of Sonny. What's wrong with you today? You used to be so chipper on Thanksgiving?

MARIE It's just different this year. Don't you feel it?

JOHN (pause) Just try to have a good time. Sean and Leslie will be here soon and we'll be a family again.

He puts his arm around her.

MARIE (pulling away) Space.

JOHN Sorry.

*John exits into the kitchen. Marie snaps a linen over the table as the front door swings open. **SEAN ANDERSON**, 20s, a muscular all American guy, enters with a backpack and a duffel bag that reads: U.C. BERKLEY WATER POLO.*

SEAN Hey Mom.

Marie jumps from being startled.

MARIE Geez, Sean!! You scared the crap out of me.

Sean crosses and hugs his mother. She pulls away quickly.

MARIE Where's your sister?

SEAN She's running late.

MARIE (slight panic) What time is she going to be here?

SEAN I don't know. She just dropped me off and went to pick up Chet. She also wanted to get you some flowers.

MARIE I don't want last minute grocery store flowers! They're all wrapped up in that noisy plastic and soaking wet! You spend half the time trying to pick off that gooey price tag to make it look like you didn't buy them at a grocery store. (beat) I hope they come with a packet of that powder stuff you put in the water. I once had a bouquet of ranunculus last for 16 weeks.

SEAN Mom, you okay?

MARIE I'm fine. (calling) John where's my Dago?

John enters with a glass of red wine.

MARIE This isn't chardonnay.

JOHN You drank it all. (noticing Sean) Oh my gosh! Sean, I didn't see you.

They hug. It is obvious they are happy to see each other.

JOHN How's the Water Polo team? And your grades?

SEAN They're great. I'm great. (beat) I got some news to tell you later.

JOHN Honey, Sean's got news.

MARIE Bonnie's not coming?

SEAN I like Aunt Bonnie. (looking around) It's awesome to be home. I could really use a beer.

John smiles and exits into the kitchen.

MARIE When did you start drinking beer? I thought all you drank was soy milk and wheat grass smoothies!

SEAN I don't drink soy anymore. I found out it gives you tits.

MARIE Great, we got a gallon of it sitting in the fridge. (beat) Hope the cats like it.

Marie exits into the kitchen. John enters with a couple of beers.

JOHN How was your flight?

SEAN Bumpy! What's with Mom?

JOHN Bumpy! When did you start drinking beer? You don't smoke pot now too, do you?

SEAN No Dad. God, you and Mom are so wound up. What's going on around here?

John spies to see that they are alone.

JOHN It's your Mother.

SEAN She's not sick is she?

JOHN I don't know. Things are changing all the time with her. For example, one day she just decided to stop doing laundry and going to church! She's drinking a lot too.

SEAN How's her arthritis?

JOHN She needs an operation. But when I bring it up she won't even talk about it. (beat) She's afraid of not waking up after the surgery.

SEAN That's ridiculous.

JOHN That's what I tell her!

Marie enters with place mats and napkins.

MARIE My ears are burning.

JOHN We were talking about Sean's team.

SEAN Yeah, about one of my friends who has arthritis. He could get an operation to fix the problem, but he's afraid he won't wake up from the anesthetic. Isn't that stupid?

Marie stares sternly at Sean for a beat, then...

MARIE Who remembers how to fold a napkin to look like a goose?

She attempts to fold one.

JOHN I can do a sailors knot.

MARIE Terrific. I'll remember that if we invite the Coast Guard.

SEAN I can fold them the way I used to at the restaurant.

MARIE Thank you.

Sean folds napkins as Marie drags John into the living room.

MARIE What have you been telling him?

JOHN Nothing.

MARIE (lighting a cigarette) For crying outloud, John! I just want to have a nice meal and catch up on my kids. I don't want to play dodge Mommy's issues between pass me the yams!

She storms off into the kitchen.

SEAN Sorry Dad.

JOHN It doesn't matter Sean. (smiling) I'm in trouble a lot these days.

The doorbell rings.

JOHN There's your sister.

He crosses to the front door, it's **CHET**, *30s, preppy and perfectly dressed in Ralph Lauren. He has a cheap bottle of red wine and a box of chocolates.*

CHET Happy Thanksgiving Mr. Anderson.

JOHN Chet, you don't have to ring the bell. And would you stop calling me Mr. Anderson. You earned that privilege when you married my daughter. (looking outside) Where is Leslie?

CHET Parking the Rover. Looks like snow. I hear it's supposed to get down in the twenties tonight. Oh, these are for you and Mrs. Anders...uh, Marie.

JOHN (half smile) Oh, a bottle of Cranes Merlot and a Whitman Sampler.

CHET All chews! I 'sampled' a couple on the way over. Sorry, low blood sugar.

Chet crosses to Sean.

CHET Hey Sean, how's Berkley? Got a girlfriend yet?

SEAN Hello Chet. (holding up a napkin) You know how to fold a goose?

LESLIE, *late 20s, a natural beauty, fumbles with an apple pie, a bouquet of flowers and a brown paper bag with beer inside.*

JOHN (rushing to her) Happy Thanksgiving. Apple I hope.

LESLIE (flustered) Thanks Dad. Yeah, it's apple. Where's Mom?

Marie enters from the kitchen and crosses to the front door, closing it.

MARIE You know, the heat is on. John take that stuff into the kitchen. Is that pie? I hope it's not apple.

Leslie looks at Sean and rolls her eyes.

MARIE Hello Chet, Happy Thanksgiving. How's the hospital? Any gory stories you want to get out of the way before we sit down to eat?

John exits into the kitchen.

LESLIE Sorry we're late Mom. I meant to come by earlier to help. But I couldn't pry someone away from the football game.

MARIE Well, it's a good thing I saved plenty for you to do. I feel so unorganized this year. Do you know I haven't even started the biscuit mix yet.

SEAN Tragedy.

MARIE I'll remind you of that smart ass when you're looking for something to sop up your gravy!

Leslie takes off her coat and sets her purse and keys down.

LESLIE Just use the pop and fresh kind.

MARIE Oh, I hate those. It's like clubbing a baby seal and watching the doughy brains pop out.

(beat) Can you help me in the kitchen?

LESLIE If you don't smoke in there.

MARIE It's my kitchen, I'll do what the hell I want.

LESLIE Fine Mother.

Marie and Leslie cross to the kitchen.

CHET Hey Les, would you bring me a micro-brew?

LESLIE Do you think you should? You're on call tonight at the hospital.

CHET I know. I'm a big boy, I know my limits.

Chet fiddles with his hospital pager as Leslie exits into the kitchen.

SEAN I would think this would be a big holiday for gastroenterologists.

CHET Actually, Passover is bigger.

SEAN Why Gastro, Chet? I mean, of ALL the different choices of doctors, you choose the ass!

CHET (defensive) Hey, there's a lot of money up there! Hell, three endoscopies and an upper G.I. series and I'm sitting on a white sandy beach in Hawaii for two weeks!! (beat) Fact! One out of every three men WILL get colon cancer.

SEAN Good for you.

CHET You betcha. I do a little happy dance every time they build another McDonalds!

Sean glares at Chet.

CHET (defensive) Hey, I don't tell people what to eat.

Chet crosses into the kitchen. Sean finishes the napkins, then crosses to a wall of photographs, old and new.

SEAN (calling out) Mom, is this picture of me and Leslie at Uncle Burl's funeral new?

MARIE (O.S.) Yes, I found a box full of old negatives in the attic.

SEAN (smiling) Negatives. (beat) Do you ever use that digital camera we gave you last Christmas?

Marie enters with a tray of glasses.

MARIE No, it's still in the box. That thing makes me nervous.

SEAN I know. That one cord you plug in to your USB can be daunting.

MARIE See right there. What's a USB? (beat) Your father and I are old school. You know that.

SEAN It's so easy to use. You just plug it into...

MARIE Sean, please don't start in on me about being behind the times.

SEAN (changing the subject) I'm sorry, never mind. Who's in this picture?

Marie crosses to him.

MARIE That's Aunt Bonnie's second husband, Henderson.

SEAN What happened to him?

MARIE No one knows. He went to Atlantic City one weekend with the Rotarians and never came home. (beat) Of course, I have my own ideas of what happened to him.

SEAN What?

MARIE I shouldn't say... (beat) Hookers and hand jobs. Aunt Bonnie found out and...

Marie makes a gun out of her hand and puts it to her head.

SEAN Really?

MARIE I'm just saying.

SEAN Harsh. Mom, I may be having a friend over to stay the night. That's okay, isn't it?

MARIE I guess. We can move Aunt Bonnie down into the basement and give your friend...

SEAN Michael.

MARIE (beat) Michael, her room.

SEAN It's really musty down there. I can sleep there.

MARIE She's used to that climate. Besides, she won't stink up the house that way. (beat) Do I know this Michael?

SEAN No. You want me to set the silverware?

MARIE It's all I've ever wanted.

Marie lights a cigarette exiting into the kitchen.

LESLIE (O.S.) MOM! Really?

Sean smiles as Marie quickly comes back into the room.

MARIE I forgot! I promised your sister I wouldn't smoke in my kitchen. All these damn rules in my own house. You can sure tell when the kids are home! (beat) Could you go into the kitchen and get my glass of wine for me. It's sitting next to that bottle of cheap crap Chet brought.

Sean exits as the doorbell rings. Marie looks at her watch.

MARIE Dear God, no one's supposed to be here for two more hours!

She crosses to the door as John enters.

JOHN Was that the doorbell?

Marie opens the front door, pauses, then slams it.

MARIE It's your brother Sonny, he's early again this year.

She heads off to the kitchen. Passing Sean, she grabs the wine and exits. John opens the door. It's UNCLE SONNY, 46, a bit soft around the edges with a warm smile and his husband, LAVELLE, who is an effeminate black man in his 40's. He carries a canned ham, Sonny, a sopping wet bouquet of grocery store flowers. They BOTH wear matching Rainbow Pride winter scarves.

JOHN Come on in out of the cold. You caught Marie off guard, you're early.

John grabs their luggage off the porch and closes the door.

LAVELLE I told you Sonny. We should have had the taxi driver circle the block a few times.

SONNY Should we come back later?

LAVELLE And just where are we supposed to go? It's Thanksgiving, the only thing open is Chinese restaurants! Although a duck dum dow sounds wonderful right know. I'm starving.

(beat) Hello John.

They hug. LaVelle hands him the canned ham.

LAVELLE They were giving them away at work.

JOHN Thank you LaVelle. We love canned ham. (beat) I'll put it in the tornado shelter. (beat)

Well, make yourself at home.

John crosses and takes Sonny's coat.

JOHN Happy Thanksgiving, Sonny. I'm glad you made it out. I can't believe it's been a whole year.

Sonny and John hug. LaVelle crosses to Sean.

LAVELLE Hello, Sean. How's college?

SEAN Great LaVelle. Congratulations on you and Uncle Sonny getting married.

LAVELLE Well, I had to do it before he couldn't fit into a wedding dress anymore!

LaVelle explodes into laughter as Marie enters with a small relish tray.

MARIE I threw this relish tray together since you're early. The real appetizers will be here when the rest of the guests arrive... (beat)...on time!

She sets the tray on the coffee table, then exits.

LAVELLE And hello to you too! I told you she'd be upset.

SONNY (sotto) Okay, okay. You're right.

JOHN You two get comfortable.

Sonny and LaVelle go to the couch as John heads upstairs with their coats and luggage.

Chet enters with a beer and crosses to Sean.

CHET (to Sean) I see the fairies flew in. (beat) God, it makes me sick to my stomach to think about those two!

SEAN Maybe you should see a gastroenterologist.

CHET Ha, ha! I mean it! It's not right. Two men being married like normal people. What ever happened to sanctity of marriage?

SEAN Dude, really?   It was replaced with divorce!

CHET Don't tell Leslie I said anything about the gays, I'm supposed to be accepting the fact that not everyone is like me. (beat) It isn't easy.

SEAN Why do you care, Chet?

CHET What?

SEAN Why do you give a crap what someone does in the privacy of their own home?

CHET Huh?

SEAN How do you have time to do your residency at the hospital and worry about gay marriage too?

CHET I make the time!

SEAN Okay, good chat Chet.

Sean crosses to his duffel bag and hikes it upstairs.

Marie enters and crosses to Sonny and LaVelle, who are looking through a pack of photos.

MARIE You both like nuts.

She tosses a can of unopened mixed nuts on the coffee table.

SONNY Marie, I brought some prints from last Thanksgiving.

He hands a few to her. She flips through them, stopping at one.

MARIE (smirking) Chet, you're wearing the same clothes as last year!

CHET Huh?

LAVELLE I didn't want to say anything.

John comes from downstairs.

JOHN Who needs a drink?

SONNY I'll have a beer. LaVelle?

LAVELLE Cream soda, honey. Do you have any cream soda?

MARIE No. How many people do you know that just happen to have cream soda in their fridge? We have Pepsi, beer, wine and a hell of a lot milk.

LAVELLE Coke Zero?

MARIE Did I say Coke Zero?

Marie crosses to the dining table shaking her head.

SONNY Come on LaVelle, I'll find you something.

John, Sonny and LaVelle exit into the kitchen.

Chet crosses to the TV turning on the football game.

He sits on the couch unbuttoning his Polo sweater and fiddling with his pager.

Leslie enters with a stack of plates.

LESLIE Chet, you're not watching football already?

Chet throws her a disapproving glance as they set the table.

LESLIE Why does he do that? At least he could offer to help.

MARIE He used to. (beat) When you two first started dating he was plenty helpful.

LESLIE You mean like when he got me pregnant?

MARIE I don't think I knew that.

LESLIE (beat) Oops.

MARIE Anything else you want to spill? (looking the table over) What's missing?

The phone rings, Marie crosses to answer.

MARIE Hello? Happy Thanksgiving to you...who is this? Hold on. (loudly) Sean, there's a Michael on the phone for you.

SEAN (O.S.) I'll take it upstairs. (beat) Okay, I got it.

Marie stays on the line a little longer than she should before hanging up. She crosses back to the table.

Chet jumps back into his seat.

CHET (loudly) Aww, come on! That was totally interference!

LESLIE Chet! No one cares. (to Marie) Who was that on the phone?

MARIE Michael, a friend of your brother's. You dated three different 'Michaels' didn't you?

LESLIE Yes, and you disapproved of all of them.

MARIE For good reason, Michael number one was a slob. Michael number two sniffed his fingers and Michael number three had a lazy...

LESLIE Okay, okay I get it.

MARIE Well, now you bagged a butt doctor, so all's good in the world.

LaVelle comes out of the kitchen, followed by Sonny and John.

LAVELLE Where's my coat? I'm going to 7-11 for a cream soda.

SONNY I'll get the coats. We'll be right back, John. How long before dinners ready, Marie?

MARIE Shortly after the time you were supposed to arrive.

JOHN Wait a minute, I'll drive you to the store.

MARIE No, you won't. You have to get the folding chairs down from the attic. Chet can take them.

LESLIE Yeah, he's NOT doing anything!

Sonny runs upstairs for their coats. John crosses to Chet.

JOHN Chet, would you do me a favor and run Sonny and LaVelle to the store?

CHET What? The Cowboys are fourth and goal!

LESLIE (sternly) Chet, that stupid game will be on when you get back.

CHET But...

Leslie gives him the 'eye.'

CHET Okay, let's go. Where are the keys?

LESLIE In my purse. Bring me a People magazine and a Kit-Kat.

MARIE I need cigarettes.

CHET Geez, anyone else need anything?

MARIE I'll check.

Marie crosses and picks up the phone.

MARIE Sean, excuse me for interrupting. Do you need anything from 7-11? We're making a run. Okay. (hanging up) A toothbrush.

Sonny comes downstairs. Chet grabs Leslie's purse and walks out.

CHET Let's go.

Sonny and LaVelle cross to the front door putting on their coats.

SONNY See you in a jiffy. (beat) Oh, it's really cold out there.

LAVELLE This is why I want to live in California!

LaVelle raises his plucked eyebrows up and down with a big smile. They exit.

LAVELLE (O.S.) Oh Chet, I love your purse.

CHET (O.S.) Hardy har har, LaVelle.

LESLIE Why do people always pick on my husband?

MARIE (beat) You really want me to answer that?

LESLIE No.

MARIE You're welcome. Now, please get the candles. (to John) And you get the folding chairs.

Leslie exits into the kitchen, John upstairs.

MARIE I used to love the holidays. When did they become so much work?

Marie lights a cigarette, then spies the phone. She slowly picks up the receiver and starts to listen as she is startled by Leslie entering with the candles. She slams the phone down.

LESLIE Mom!!?? Were you trying to listen to Sean on the phone?

MARIE No!! I, I was going to page Chet and tell him to...bring me some...uh...eye drops.

LESLIE Yeah, right.

MARIE You don't believe me. That hurts. (beat) I got to baste the turkey.

She exits into the kitchen as Sean comes downstairs.

SEAN Was that you screwing with the phone?

LESLIE No, that was Mom. She was trying to listen to your conversation, but I walked in on her.

SEAN Why would she do that? I'm telling you something weird is going on with her.

LESLIE What do you mean?

SEAN Don't you notice it?

LESLIE Let's not talk about Mom. I see her all the time. Sometimes I wish we didn't live so close. (beat) Gosh, that's a crappy thing to say.

SEAN It's okay, I know what you mean. (beat) It's really great to be with you Leslie. I miss you. I know we talk on the phone a lot, but...

LESLIE A lot? I got a two hundred dollar phone bill last month. Chet went through the roof.

SEAN How are you two doing?

LESLIE Okay. (long pause) Shitty! (pause) He's at that damn hospital all the time. Somewhere between work and sleep, he forgets about me. (beat) Things aren't good right now, Sean. I think we are going to try counseling.

SEAN Sorry, Les.

Leslie shrugs her shoulders, but looks like she is going to cry.

SEAN (smiling) Hey, did you start your Christmas shopping yet? You are never going to guess what I got you!

Leslie perks back up.

LESLIE (proudly) I started the day after Halloween! I'm all done except I still don't know what I'm going to get Chet.

SEAN He's a hard one. I mean how can you beat last year? Adopting him a milking Goat in Uganda is pretty hard to top!

They laugh as John struggles downstairs with some folding chairs.

SEAN Dad, let me help.

JOHN Thanks Sean.

Sean takes a couple of chairs and puts them at the table. John follows.

JOHN I hate going up in the attic. I got bit by a spider.

He shows Sean his left hand. On the back of it is a big red welt.

SEAN (concerned) Dad, your hand is really swollen! What kind of spider was it?

JOHN I don't know, brown. (rubbing his hand) I must have startled it.

Leslie jumps up.

LESLIE Dad, let me see.

SEAN Let's get some ice.

LESLIE Dad, come over here and sit down.

She leads him to the couch. Sean exits into the kitchen.

JOHN Would you two stop worrying. You know how allergic I am to this kind of thing, everything. I pricked my finger on one of your mother's rose bushes, and it ballooned up like a thermometer! Don't worry, the swelling will be gone in an hour.

LESLIE I know, but remember what happen when you got stung by those wasps? Let's just put some ice on it.

Marie enters with a baggie of ice followed by Sean. She is very concerned, but reserved.

MARIE John, let me see where you got bit.

She takes his hand gingerly.

MARIE Do you need your inhaler?

JOHN No Marie, I'm fine. Really honey, I feel okay.

MARIE Are you sure? Should I call Dr. Smiff?

LESLIE Yeah Mom, call Dr. Smiff!

JOHN (sternly) I'm fine everyone. Now please stop fussing over me.

He kisses Marie on the cheek and goes upstairs. Leslie exits into the kitchen.

Marie wipes off her cheek.

SEAN Is dad really, okay?

MARIE (beat) Sure.

Sean smiles and. goes upstairs.

SEAN I'll be in my room.

Marie takes a cigarette out of her apron, lights it and crosses into the kitchen. After a moment...

LESLIE (O.S.) Mom!!

George Winston's 'FRAGRANT FIELDS," from the Summer album, *begins to play.*

The stage sits empty for a moment until a soft knock comes from the front door. Another knock, then another and another...

Slowly the door opens. ***AUNT BONNIE***, *a frail women in her 80's, leans on a walker. Her crooked silhouette stands in the doorway.*

She slowly enters the house. She has hearing aids and a nasal cannula in her nose. Behind her, a small, stern, ***JAPANESE NURSE*** *has a large carpet bag over her shoulder. Under her arm, is a folding screen. She pulls* *an oxygen tank behind Bonnie making her look like an organ grinders monkey!*

Nurse leaves Bonnie for a moment to set up her M.A.S.H unit in the living room.

She then places Bonnie slowly and methodically in a chair, then takes out a blanket, pillow, special cup with a straw, diapers, numerous pill bottles and a blood pressure cuff out of the carpet bag.

Once satisfied that everything is in order, she takes out a crossword book, and sits.

*The **MUSIC** ends.*

Marie enters with some wicker baskets as Bonnie suddenly explodes with a horrendous sneeze.

MARIE (screaming) OH MY GOD!!!

Marie tosses the wicker baskets in the air.

MARIE Bonnie! You scared the crap out of me.

BONNIE Well, I guess you can thank me for losing ten pounds! (beat) This is my Asian Nurse. I wanted an American, but this is all they had.

NURSE I am an American!

BONNIE Maybe on your fake green card, but you're not fooling me! (beat) I hate having a nurse, but I can't wipe my own butt anymore.

Isn't that a shame?

NURSE Only for me.

MARIE (to Nurse) Well, welcome to our home. I hope you like Thanksgiving turkey.

BONNIE She's not eating with us. She's working.

Nurse rolls her eyes and goes back to her crossword.

BONNIE (to Nurse) Give her the thing.

NURSE The thing?

BONNIE Yeah, you know, the thing. The damn gift, and the other thing!

NURSE The food?

BONNIE Give them to me.

Nurse pulls a wrapped present and a foil covered pan out of her bag.

BONNIE Marie, I brought my favorite dish. (to Nurse) Give her the pan. (to Marie)

All the way from Florida.

Nurse hands the dish to Marie.

MARIE Florida? Well, whatever it is, it doesn't need to be refrig-
erated.

BONNIE (to Nurse) Turn up my air, damn it.

Nurse fiddles with the tank valve.

BONNIE More. (beat) That's good. (she takes a deep couple of breaths)

Marie peaks under the foil.

BONNIE You know I don't cook but I wanted to bring something.
They make these every week in the cafetorium at the 'Acres.' I had
them whip me up a batch to bring here. Caramelized Dwarf Pears in
heavy syrup.

MARIE Mmmmm. (sotto) Sounds horrid.

BONNIE What?

MARIE What?

BONNIE We like them down at the home because you don't need
your teeth to chew them. Speaking of that...

Bonnie pulls out her upper teeth and hands them to Nurse.

BONNIE Nurse, give these a whirl around the Efferdent. Feel a little
gritty after that long flight.

NURSE I'm not touching those nasty things.

Nurse grimaces at the dripping dentures, then reluctantly goes through the routine of cleaning them with a tooth brush.

BONNIE (to Nurse) Don't make that face. It's not my fault you weren't smart enough to choose something else to do with your short life. (to Marie) All that time on the boat ride over to this country to figure out what to do, and she chooses to work with senior citizens. What does that tell you?

MARIE Well Bonnie, make yourself comfortable. I'm going to put these dwarves in the kitchen, get a room deodorizer and let everyone know that your here.

Marie exits as John comes down stairs.

JOHN Aunt Bonnie!!! I'm so glad you made it.

BONNIE I'm so glad I make it anywhere these days, John.

JOHN Happy Thanksgiving.

John expertly gives Bonnie a hug, navigating through the tubes and paraphernalia.

BONNIE How's my favorite nephew?

JOHN Great. It's nice to have everyone home.

Bonnie surveys the room.

BONNIE Looks like I'm it, buster. This is my Nurse. She's a Japanese.

JOHN Welcome to our home. 'Watashi tachi no ie e yo koso.'

NURSE 'Omaneki itadaki arigato gozaimasu.'

BONNIE (to Nurse) If you are done with the gibberish, I'd like to have my teeth back in my mouth!

Nurse places the last bit of adhesive on the dentures and hands them to Bonnie.

BONNIE Put them in my mouth.

NURSE I'm not putting them in your mouth. That's where I draw the line.

BONNIE Really? Since when do you get to decide where the line is drawn?

NURSE Since I control your bank account! Now, put your teeth back in your mouth and be quiet!

John looks away not knowing what to say. Bonnie, sheepishly takes the dentures and puts them in her mouth.

NURSE (big smile) Ha, ha, ha! Just kidding!

BONNIE Yes, you are. A riot. You should do a comedy tour. (to John) You get my post card? You know I moved.

JOHN Marie mentioned something. Do you like your new home?

BONNIE John, I live in a place called 'Lazy Acres'. You tell me, would you like that?

JOHN Well...

BONNIE What's forty feet long and smells like urine?

JOHN Uh, I don't know.

BONNIE A conga line at a senior citizen's home!!

Nurse laughs. John looks horrified as Bonnie yanks on her cannula.

BONNIE Turn up my air you stingy bitch! (beat) And stop laughing. You sound like an air raid siren. (beat) Give him the thing.

Nurse hands a present to John. She notices his hand.

NURSE Your hand is swollen.

JOHN Spider bite.

NURSE Looks bad. I have some unguent.

BONNIE Don't worry about his damn hand! Give him the envelopes.

Nurse removes two thick envelopes from her bag. They each have a small bow stuck on them.

BONNIE That's them. Something for Sean and Leslie. Where the hell are they?

JOHN Sean's upstairs and Leslie's helping Marie in the kitchen. They'll be so excited to see you.

BONNIE That's good because the only one excited to see me lately is Donny the mortician at Valhalla Bros. I bought my plot last week.

BONNIE (to John) You got your plots picked out?

JOHN Uh, not yet. I think we want to be cremated.

BONNIE Think? Kind of a big decision to be on the fence about. I was hoping you and Marie could be buried on top of me.

NURSE Gross.

BONNIE That's not what I meant nosey Nurse. (beat) I'm thirsty, and I can't breathe! Are we on air rationing today? Turn the damn switch up, I feel like I'm inhaling through a shoebox.

Nurse turns up the air and goes about pouring juice into a special cup. The front door opens swiftly. Chet walks straight to the TV, turning it on. The SFX of the football game resume. Sonny enters with an empty Slurpee cup, followed by LaVelle carrying a bag.

LAVELLE Don't pout Sonny. It's not my fault you sucked it all down on the way home.

BONNIE Oh, good, the gays are here!

JOHN Bonnie has arrived, everyone.

NURSE Hip Hip Hooray!

Bonnie shoots Nurse a look.

LAVELLE Happy Thanksgiving, Bonnie. Nice to see you again.

Chet throws a wave in the air. Sonny crosses to her as LaVelle exits into the kitchen. Bonnie stares at LaVelle.

BONNIE Who's the Black guy? Is this a new boyfriend?

SONNY LaVelle and I got married.

He shows off his ring.

BONNIE Oh yeah, you can do that now.

CHET Not in the red states.

SONNY LaVelle was here last year. Don't you remember?

BONNIE He looks familiar.

CHET Not too many Black guys coming through this house, not hard to forget.

SONNY Excuse me?

JOHN Chet!?

SONNY Of course. You remember Lavelle, Bonnie.

BONNIE Maybe. Hell, I don't remember what I had for breakfast.

NURSE (beat) Vanilla Ensure.

CHET (a little loud) That was a crappy call. He was totally out of bounds.

NURSE His foot was on the little white line when he caught the ball.

Chet looks back over his shoulder, confused.

CHET What? Uh…what do you know about football?

NURSE I know enough to admit when I'm wrong.

Nurse smiles blankly at Chet, then goes back to her crossword.

CHET (irritated) Nurses!

Leslie enters with a tray of appetizers. Bonnie falls to sleep in her chair.

LESLIE Warm nibbles.

CHET Bring them over here, Les.

Leslie crosses to Chet and sets the tray down. He pops a stuffed mushroom in his mouth. Chet fans his mouth.

CHET (mumbled) HEY! These are hot! You should have warned me.

LESLIE Oh, sorry. (smiling) Watch out, the mushrooms are hot. (beat) When did Aunt Bonnie get here?

CHET (chewing) I don't know. But it smells like the geriatric ward in here now.

LESLIE Chet, be nice.

John crosses to Sonny.

JOHN So, how you been little brother?

Sonny looks over John's shoulder, then pulls a folded letter out of his jacket pocket.

SONNY Things are okay, John. (sotto) I got a letter from the Priest at my church. He informed me that my services as organ player will no longer be needed.

JOHN What? Why? You've been playing there for years.

SONNY (sadly) Because I'm gay.

John's expression goes blank as he sits on the arm of a chair.

JOHN But you've always been gay. Even before you played the organ. Why do they care now?

SONNY It's Father Finnigan. He says I'm an abomination.

JOHN But you were there before Father Finnigan. I don't understand. Can't the Elders do something about it?

SONNY (angry) It's so unfair. It means so much to me. (beat) Why does he care? Why does anybody care about my sexuality? (pause) How can I watch someone else play that organ? I was the one who helped raise the money to buy it in the first place! (beat) I don't understand religion. Wasn't I a good steward? Didn't I dedicate every Wednesday and Sunday to the Perish? LaVelle is beside himself. We can't even talk about it because he gets so upset. (beat) He even wrote a nasty letter to the Pope and one to Dr. Phil!

LaVelle enters with a cream soda and a People magazine. He sits on a high stool at the bar.

JOHN I'm sorry, Sonny. I wish there was something I could do.

SONNY (smiling) You could punch Father Finnigan in the nose! (beat) But it's best to turn a cheek, I guess.

Sonny wipes the tears away. LaVelle, noticing, crosses to them.

LAVELLE You told him?

Sonny nods his head 'yes.'

LAVELLE It's a damn shame. Sonny is the finest organist in the community. I'm afraid he's played his last Amazing Grace in that dump! I'll never set foot in that Church again!

SONNY LaVelle, you shouldn't let the opinion of one man, keep you away from your worship.

LAVELLE Oh honey, it goes a lot deeper than that. Besides, I don't need a building to have a relationship with God. Can I get an Amen?

(beat)

It's Thanksgiving so let's put all of that aside for today. (beat) Have you told John the good news?

JOHN (smiling) What good news?

Sonny turns away blushing.

LAVELLE Oh, for goodness' sake Sonny, tell him!

John's eyes widen as he breaks into a huge smile.

JOHN You're in a show!

After a beat, Sonny explodes with excitement.

SONNY YES!!!

John and LaVelle cheer as Chet, turns up the volume on the TV.

CHET Shush!

JOHN What show? And please don't make me guess...

Suddenly Sonny and LaVelle break into song, complete with harmonies.

LAVELLE Five, six, seven and eight...

SONNY / LAVELLE "WE KNOW WE BELONG TO THE LAND AND THE LAND WE BELONG TO IS GRAND! AND WE SAY, YO, I YIP I YO YEE YAY. WE'RE ONLY SAYIN' YOU'RE DOING FINE..."

CHET OKLAHOMO!

SONNY/LAVELLE "O-K-L-A-H-O-M-A, OKLAHOMA. YEOW!!

Sonny and LaVelle end with a dramatic pose. John and Leslie clap as Chet shakes his head in disgust. Bonnie stirs awake in her chair.

CHET (sotto) This is why our country is going down the drain!

LAVELLE My Sonny's the lead! John, your brother is playing Curly. The handsome cowboy stud.

LaVelle kisses Sonny as Chet yanks his hospital pager off his belt.

CHET (sotto) Please beep. Get me out of here. I'd rather be inside a colon. Please beep!

LESLIE Curly! That's great Uncle Sonny.

SONNY (chuckling) They're using a lot of makeup and pushing the audience back twenty feet.

LESLIE I love that musical. My drama department did it when I was in high school.

LAVELLE Do a song Sonny. Sing "People Will Say We're in Love." I'll do the girl's part.

CHET Figures!

LESLIE Chet, shut up. Go ahead Uncle sonny.

LAVELLE I've got the libretto in my bag.

SONNY (embarrassed) He makes me rehearse in the car too.

LAVELLE Well, there's only five weeks before we open.

LESLIE Are you in the show too, LaVelle?

LAVELLE I'm on the hair and makeup crew. I'm taking a sabbatical from acting. That's how Sonny and I met, you know. We were both in Annie. I played FDR.

SONNY It was Annie junior, actually.

JOHN I don't know that musical.

BONNIE (groggy) Yes you do. It's that stupid show about that idiotic little red head and some bald Perv.

NURSE It ran on Broadway for years and made a fortune. The real Annie, not Annie junior.

BONNIE How the hell do you know anything about any Annie?

NURSE I'm a theater nerd. I also saw Les Miserable at the National Theater of Tokyo. Kimura Takuya was brilliant as Jean Valjean.

BONNIE You're a nerd alright! No one cares. (beat) So, Sonny, you going to butcher a song or what? If you are, I need to take out my hearing aids.

SONNY I don't think so Bonnie. Maybe later.

BONNIE At my age honey, there may not be a later, thank God.

JOHN Come on Sonny, it'll be fun.

They all start to egg Sonny into performing. As they get louder, Chet turns up the TV.

CHET Could you keep it down, I'm trying to watch the game.

Marie enters. She watches for a beat, then shouts.

MARIE I'm really glad everybody wants Sonny to sing, but the Cabaret is closed! (beat) I could really use some help in the kitchen. Otherwise, we won't be eating until midnight.

BONNIE Midnight!? Then why the hell did we get here so early?

LESLIE I'll help you, Mom.

SONNY Me too.

Leslie, Marie and Sonny exit into the kitchen. John joins Chet on the couch. Lavelle crosses to Bonnie.

LAVELLE We got your postcard. Lazy Acres... (beat) ...looks nice.

BONNIE Who you fooling? It's a damn prison with bingo and a therapy pool.

LAVELLE My mother's in assisted living care too. She has dementia. I don't see her much and when I do, she doesn't know who I am.

BONNIE That sounds nice.

LaVelle gives her an odd look as Bonnie grimaces and shifts back and forth in her chair.

NURSE (putting down the crossword) Is it time?

BONNIE Soon. Don't worry, you'll be the first to know!

NURSE That would be helpful, we don't need another accident.

Sean comes bouncing downstairs checking his cell phone.

SEAN Did anyone call for me?

JOHN No Sean.

SEAN Hey Aunt Bonnie, Happy Thanksgiving.

As he hugs her gently, she recoils back.

SEAN What did I do? Did I hurt you?

BONNIE No honey, my hearing aid buzzes when people or Asians get too close.

Nurse throws her a look.

BONNIE Sean, I have something for you and your sister later. (to John) Where did you put those envelopes?

JOHN They're over here Aunt Bonnie.

He holds up the envelopes.

SEAN Cool. I can't wait.

Without warning, Bonnie, wide eyed springs up in her chair.

BONNIE Well, you might have to, I need to go to the bathroom!! (to Nurse) Quick, set me up.

NURSE Number one or number two.

BONNIE I think it's going to be a thirteen!

NURSE Code blue!

Nurse goes into action. LaVelle gets a strange look on his face.

LAVELLE I'll see if there's anything I can do in the kitchen.

He bolts from the room. Sean, not sure what to do, makes his way to the couch.

The others try to ignore the Albatross in the room. Chet turns up the volume on the TV. Nurse crosses and sets up the folding screen in front of Bonnie blocking her view from the audience.

Leslie enters and crosses to John and Sean.

Nurse snaps on a pair of rubber gloves, picks up her large bag and crosses to the screen.

NURSE I'm going in. See you on the other side.

Nurse bows to them, then goes behind the screen. Sean, Leslie and John watch in disbelief.

SEAN (hushed) Dad, I don't ever want to be like that. You know, not being able to do things for myself.

JOHN (hushed) I don't think Aunt Bonnie wanted to end up like this.

LESLIE (hushed) I feel so uncomfortable around her. Dad, how do you act so normal?

JOHN I just try and remember her the way she used to be. (beat) You know kids, if your mother and I ever get sick, please take care of us. I mean, I don't want to be a burden, but I don't want to be put in some hospital room where all I do is watch TV and wait to die.

LESLIE Dad, we would never do that.

SEAN Chet might.

Leslie playfully slaps Sean as Marie enters agitated. She notices the screen around Bonnie and crosses to it.

MARIE (angry) What the HELL is this??

BONNIE It's a puppet show! You'd better get a good seat; the performance is about to start. (beat) Do you mind Marie? I'm trying to go to the bathroom!

MARIE I'm very sorry. For a moment I thought this was my living room not a public toilet.

Nurse sticks her head out. She's holding a rubber hose of some kind.

NURSE Could you please not talk to her. We're trying to concentrate and timing is crucial. Thank you.

She bows her head then ducks back behind the screen.

MARIE Now I've seen, or haven't seen everything.

Disgusted, Marie retreats to the kitchen.

CHET Go for the two-point conversion. Geez, what an A-hole!!

John rubs his hand then shakes it out.

SEAN Dad, did you show Chet your hand?

JOHN No, it feels fine. Just a little numb.

CHET What's wrong with your hand?

JOHN Nothing, I got bit by a spider.

CHET What kind of spider?

JOHN I don't know, a spider, spider.

CHET Let me see.

John reluctantly shows Chet his hand.

CHET (smiling) Hey, this one's free.

Chet looks at his swollen hand all the time keeping one eye on the game.

CHET Take some aspirin and if it's not better, call a doctor in the morning. (chuckling) I've always wanted to say that. Rest a cold beer bottle on it.

LESLIE Really Chet? That's all you got?

Leslie, shakes her head as she goes to the front door.

LESLIE I need some air.

She takes a long hard look at Chet, grabs her coat, then goes outside.

CHET (confused) What did I do? (frustrated) I'm going to get another beer.

Chet heads for the kitchen as LaVelle exits with a cream soda. He crosses to the chair where Chet had been sitting.

LAVELLE What's the score?

SEAN I didn't know you watched football?

LAVELLE You mean because I'm gay?

JOHN I don't think that's what Sean meant.

SEAN Yeah, sorry Uncle LaVelle, I didn't mean anything like that. I just remembered you're a big Hockey fan, that's all.

LAVELLE (smiling) Yeah, I played football in high school. I was a running back. Played a little Division One, too. Got offered a scholarship to play ball at IU, but I went to cosmetology school instead. Looking back, I'm not sure it was the wisest choice. (beat) It was just a different time. Back then being gay was way more challenging. Being Black AND gay AND on the Football team...well, let's just say that was more than I wanted to handle. But things are better now... (changing the subject) Anyone else getting hungry?

LaVelle dives into the appetizers as Marie enters, cigarette in hand. Chet enters right behind her.

MARIE Who's carving the turkey this year?

CHET Don't ask me. (examining his fingers) These money makers are reserved for the OR!

MARIE You weren't even on my list Chet.

JOHN I carve the turkey!

SEAN You do it every year, Dad.

Chet stands right behind LaVelle, agitated that he has sat in 'his' seat.

MARIE I just thought because of your bad back and swollen hand...

JOHN Marie!!

MARIE Sean can carve this year.

JOHN (insistent) I'm carving!

MARIE You let me know.

JOHN I just did.

Marie crosses to the folding screen. She reaches into her apron and pulls out a pine tree shaped scented air freshener and hangs it on the screen, then exits.

CHET Uh, LaVelle, Sonny wanted to see you in the kitchen.

LAVELLE Oh, okay. Thank you, Chet.

LaVelle gets up and goes into the kitchen. Chet, with a huge grin steals back 'his' chair.

JOHN That wasn't very nice, Chet.

Chet with the expression 'who cares', sips his beer.

JOHN Chet, my hand's getting sore. Should I ice or heat?

CHET I don't know. What's the score?

John sighs and exits into the kitchen. Sean watches John with concern.

SEAN (distracted) Uh...Cowboys are down 17 to 3. It's almost half time.

CHET When the hell did that happen?

SEAN When you were in the kitchen. (beat) Is my dad going to be, okay?

CHET What? Yeah, he's fine. (beat) 17 to 3? Why didn't you call me? I hate missing the action. I have some major cashola riding on this game.

SEAN Yeah? I'm in a pool at school.

CHET (laughing) That's great Sean, but I'm talking Doctor dollars here, not beer money.

SEAN What's that supposed to mean?

CHET Why do you always do that to me? Ask me what things mean. I don't know what they mean, that's just the way it is. Just watch the game. (yelling) Come on Bullock, throw a pass someone can catch for a change.

LaVelle comes out of the kitchen.

LAVELLE (loudly to Chet) Ha, Ha! Very funny Ralph Lauren. You don't own that chair! Payback's a bitch!

LaVelle throws his head in the air as he goes back into the kitchen. Sean starts to laugh.

CHET What was that supposed to mean?

SEAN I don't know. Why do you always ask me that? That's just the way it is. Just watch the game!

CHET You know Sean, one of these days you're going to need me. I don't know when that day will be, but sooner or later every man needs to see a Gastroenterologist! And when I've got my gloved hand up your ass squeezing your prostate so hard you want to cry for your Mommy, we'll see who's laughing at who!

SEAN Geez Chet, I was only joking around.

Chet sits back in his chair, smirking. Leslie comes in through the front door, shaking off the chill.

CHET How was your walk?

LESLIE Liberating.

Chet looks confused as she takes off her coat and exits into the kitchen. Nurse comes out from behind the screen holding a red bio-hazard bag full of something. She exits upstairs.

Sonny, enters with a glass of wine. He crosses to the screen.

SONNY (excited) Bonnie, Marie said you were going to do a puppet show. LaVelle and I saw 'Avenue Q' on Broadway.

Sonny goes behind the screen, then quickly steps back out. Horrified.

SONNY (embarrassed) Uh...wow...um...that's certainly not Avenue Q!

Nurse comes downstairs. She sprays a thick cloud from a can of air freshener, then goes behind the screen.

SONNY (smelling) Oranges.

Leslie and LaVelle enter from the kitchen. He crosses to the bar with a bowl of raw green beans and a colander as Leslie puts a vase of grocery store flowers on the dining table.

Sonny crosses and sits next to LaVelle. They crack beans.

The phone rings.

Nurse steps out from behind the screen with a piece of hose and a small foot powered pump. She sits down and continues her crossword puzzle as her foot operates the plastic pump.

The phone rings. Marie steps out of the kitchen. She takes a few steps then sniffs the air, making an awful face.

MARIE Anyone going to answer the phone? (sniffing) Phew, smells like someone fertilized an orange grove! (beat) At least the kitchen smells like turkey! (answering the phone) Hello? Yes, happy Thanksgiving again to you too. Sean, it's for you...it's Michael.

Sean springs off the couch and heads upstairs.

SEAN I'll take it in my room.

Marie puts the receiver to her ear. Leslie clears her throat loudly.

MARIE What? I'm just waiting for him to pick up.

SEAN (O.S.) Okay I got it, hang up.

Marie slams the phone down. She glares at Leslie, then turns to Sonny.

MARIE How did you like the puppet show?

SONNY That was mean, Marie.

Marie exits into the kitchen. Nurse stops pumping and goes behind the screen.

LESLIE Chet, what do you think about my dad's spider bite.

CHET Why does everyone keep asking me about his spider bite?. Did you see that interception? I'm going to lose a fortune.

LESLIE What does that mean? How much is a fortune?

CHET I thought we discussed this, Leslie. You don't ask me about what I do with my money and I won't ask what you do with yours.

LESLIE I think it's my right as your wife to ask how OUR money is being spent.

CHET Of course, you are. But if I choose to use some of my... (beat) 'our' money to bet on a game, it shouldn't be any concern of yours.

LESLIE (upset) What's that all about? Do you have a separate bank account? (angry) You preach at me night and day about the values of saving money, and all the time you have a slush fund behind my back? Chet, you're a hypocrite!

CHET I'm SMART is what I am! I've seen the way you can plow through money. If it makes you feel better, call it a 'rainy day' account.

LESLIE I'll call it bull, and dishonest! You are such a fool.

CHET What did I do now?

She crosses across the room.

LAVELLE (sotto to Leslie) That's telling him, girl.

SONNY (sotto) LaVelle, stay out of it.

CHET Don't make a big deal out of this. Where you going?

LESLIE Away from you!

Leslie starts to cry and runs upstairs.

CHET What's up her skirt?

Sonny and LaVelle run after her. After a few moments, Nurse steps out from behind the screen with another red bio- hazard bag and exits upstairs.

Marie enters from the kitchen.

MARIE Are the green beans done? Where the hell is everyone?

CHET Upstairs. Leslie's mad at me, again!

MARIE You probably deserved it!

Chet swigs his beer hard. Marie grabs the beans and heads back into the kitchen.

BONNIE You know Chet, you're an asshole.

CHET So are you, Bonnie!

BONNIE Yes well, I'm an old woman in bad health who's survived five husbands and lives in a death camp. I've earned the right!

CHET What are you complaining about? They left you well off.

BONNIE Money, money, money! That's all I ever hear out of your mouth. Money is NOT everything. God son, you're a doctor. Certainly, you should realize the beauty of life. The importance of health.

CHET You know, terminally ill people are so full of themselves.

BONNIE All I know is that you, for whatever reason and I don't know why, have been blessed with a truly wonderful wife and you're throwing it all away.

Chet crosses to the screen.

CHET What do you mean I'm throwing it all away? I love Leslie, she knows that.

BONNIE Then tell her every hour on the hour! I may have had five husbands, but I never had love.

CHET (sarcastic) You're breaking my heart.

BONNIE Good, because if I had my strength I'd get up and break something else!

CHET Listen Bonnie, I don't need this.

BONNIE Yes, you do. You needed it a long time ago. You obviously had parents that showered you with money instead of affection, so you're not totally to blame. But I know you're smart enough to know the difference. Don't become another divorced chump who ends up living at a Marriott Residence Inn.

CHET (smugly) I won't. Thanks for the advice.

Chet thinks for a moment, then crosses to the staircase.

CHET Leslie. Please come down here.

Sonny comes downstairs.

SONNY Leslie doesn't want to talk to you right now.

CHET She can tell me that herself.

Chet starts up the stairs as Sonny stops him.

SONNY Just let her calm down. LaVelle is with her.

Sonny puts his hand on Chet's shoulder.

CHET Get your hands off me faggot!

Chet throws Sonny to the side.

SONNY You didn't have to do that, Chet?

LaVelle comes flying down the stairs. He goes to Sonny.

LAVELLE Oh, my dear Lord. Did he hurt you?

SONNY No, LaVelle I'm okay. (beat) He didn't mean it. Honestly.

CHET The hell I didn't, Fag!

LAVELLE (angry) Stop calling him that before I beat your ass.

SONNY LaVelle stop it. Please honey, relax. (to Chet) And you!? Stop calling me faggot! (beat) I hate that word. Life is hard enough without you calling me that?

CHET (smugly) You chose this life. Get used to it.

SONNY Are you serious? That's what's wrong, Chet. (beat) We spend so much precious time trying to convince the rest of the world that this lifestyle isn't a choice. We were born this way...

(pause) I know it's hard to understand, but why would I choose to have people hate me? Lose friends? Alienate my family? (long pause) Believe me if I had a choice, I wouldn't be gay.

LAVELLE Sonny?

SONNY It's true LaVelle. (beat) I'm getting so tired of this game. Sometimes I just want to start over.

CHET So, you're not going to be gay anymore? Good luck with that.

SONNY That's not what I'm saying.

LAVELLE All I want to do today is over eat and watch the Macy's Parade. What the hell is happening here?

SONNY What I'm saying is I'm tired of the fight. (beat) The fight to get people like you Chet, to like us. To accept us.

CHET Then why do you run around half naked at gay prides screaming equal rights?

LAVELLE Listen, why don't I punch him in the face, get our luggage and we go to a hotel.

CHET I'd like to see you try it.

LaVelle sizes Chet up.

LAVELLE You want to have a go around? I may be a little light in my loafers, but I bet I could arm wrestle you to the ground.

CHET Never gonna happen.

LAVELLE Why don't you put some cash where your mouth is?

CHET (laughing) I don't want to hurt you LaVelle. I know how easily you must bruise.

LaVelle pushes his way past Sonny getting in Chet's face.

LAVELLE I don't think so!

SONNY Come on guys. LaVelle, stop it.

LAVELLE No! I want to arm wrestle this chump. What is it Chet, you afraid to touch me because I'm gay? I'm not afraid to touch you and I KNOW where your hands have been!

Chet pushes LaVelle back.

CHET Alright, let's go LaVelle.

Chet crosses to the dining table taking off his Polo sweater.

CHET Hundred dollars says you lose.

LAVELLE A thousand!

SONNY A thousand dollars? LaVelle, we're supposed to be saving for a fountain for the backyard.

LAVELLE Don't worry Boo, by the time I'm done with this Yuppie, you can have a damn pond with a waterfall! (beat) See Chet, we all have labels!

Chet clears back two table settings and sits on the downstage corner chair.

Sean comes downstairs and crosses to Sonny.

SEAN What's going on?

SONNY Oh my, they're going to arm wrestle.

SEAN Really? Awesome!

LaVelle gets comfortable in his upstage corner seat. Sonny squirts hand sanitizer on Lavelle's hands.

CHET You got the money?

LAVELLE I got the money. You got the money?

BONNIE Apparently, he's got ALL the money.

Marie and John enter.

MARIE What are you two doing to my nice table?

SEAN They're going to arm wrestle.

JOHN What?

MARIE Dirty elbows on my Martha Stewart linens? Really?

CHET Yeah, LaVelle's trying to prove something.

LAVELLE Whose dick is bigger!

SONNY LaVelle!?

Marie smiles as she lights a cigarette.

BONNIE (behind the screen) Where the hell is my Nurse? I want to see whose dick is bigger!

(calling out) Nurse, hurry up with that toilet paper, I'm about to grab a few pages out of your crossword book.

Nurse runs down from upstairs with a roll of toilet paper that trails behind her. She exits behind the screen.

Chet rolls up his sleeves.

MARIE John, go get my wine.

John exits into the kitchen.

CHET You ready, LaVelle?

MARIE No, you can't start yet. John's getting my wine.

BONNIE (behind screen) And I'm not through yet.

NURSE Shhh, concentrate.

John hurries in with her wine.

LAVELLE Are you ready to get this show on the road?

SONNY You know, you guys don't have to do this. We all know you're both men!

CHET Well, one of us.

LAVELLE I'm about to show you my manhood, chump!

CHET Save that for Sonny.

SEAN Dad, where's your camera?

JOHN Oh, yeah. Hold on you guys, I want to get my camera.

John runs to the closet. After a few steps he stops to catch his breath, he opens the closet.

LaVelle and Chet sit disappointed back in their chairs as Nurse takes down the screen.

BONNIE Dinner and a show. Now, this will be something to talk about back at the Acres.

John comes over with a camera.

CHET Let's go! Put your hand out.

They both lean up in their chairs. LaVelle grabs Chet's hand firmly.

CHET Give me your other hand.

Chet takes LaVelle's other hand locking fingers.

CHET (sarcastic) Nice nails!

MARIE You'd better not wrinkle my tablecloth.

SEAN Okay, on the count of three. Ready? One, two, THREE!

The small crowd begins to cheer as both men's bodies tense.

Hearing the commotion, Leslie comes downstairs. She is dumbfounded.

LESLIE Aunt Bonnie, what are they doing?

BONNIE Being stupid men. Can't you smell the testosterone?

NURSE They're arm wrestling. (beat) My distant cousin Tetsu Yamamoto was the founder of the first Japanese Arm-Wrestling Federation in 1930.

LESLIE I can see they are arm wrestling! Why?

JOHN I don't know. But Chet bet Lavelle a thousand dollars!

LESLIE A thousand dollars! Chet are you out of your mind?

Chet peeks over at Leslie and grimaces. LaVelle gains momentum, Chet battles back. They struggle back and forth as the rest cheer them on.

CHET Maybe, I should have thought this through. I'm not sure how this is going to turn out.

LAVELLE I do!

LaVelle slams Chet's arm onto the table with a 'thud'!

SEAN The winner!

Sean grabs LaVelle's arm throwing it in the air like a prize fighter.

SONNY (glowing) Wow. I know exactly what fountain I want. It has two chubby cherubs riding on the back of majestic lime stone Llamas.

LAVELLE Lovely, Sonny. I'll take my money, Chet.

CHET You'll get your money.

Chet defeated, crosses to the couch, rubbing his shoulder. Leslie sits next him.

CHET I can't believe I lost to a...to him.

LESLIE A thousand dollars? You know the gambling has got to stop Chet.

CHET (pause) I'm sorry Les, you're right. I'll try to be more considerate of our money. It won't be easy, I've always been spoiled.

LESLIE Yes, you are. But that's no excuse. (beat) No more gambling though, right?

CHET No more after the football game. I promise. I'm really sorry, Les. (beat) I love you.

Leslie slides her arm around him.

LESLIE I love you too. (sternly) But I'm serious, Chet. No more gambling!

CHET I know.

Leslie and Chet sit in silence and watch the game. It's a nice moment.

Sonny rubs LaVelle's shoulders at the dining table.

SONNY I'm so proud of you LaVelle. I had no idea how strong you were.

LAVELLE Really? Who always gets all the boxes of Department 56 down out of the garage at Christmas?

SONNY You do.

LAVELLE And who always gets on the big ladder to put up the twinkle lights?

SONNY You do. You're such a stud. (sotto) I'm kind of turned on right now.

BONNIE Oh my God! That's disgusting. Nurse, turn down my hearing aids.

Suddenly there is a LOUD EXPLOSION with POPPING NOISES coming from the kitchen. Smoke starts to creep out from under the kitchen door and shutters over the bar.

MARIE What the hell!?

John, Marie, Sean, Sonny and LaVelle exit hastily into the kitchen.

NURSE It smells like burnt popcorn.

BONNIE Oh good, you smell it too. I thought I was having a stroke!

MARIE (O.S.) (hysterical) MY TURKEY! John what happened to the turkey?

JOHN (O.S.) Be careful opening the stove, Marie.

SONNY (O.S.) John look out!

BOOM!! SPLAT!! The sounds of a something horrible hitting the floor are heard.

MARIE (O.S.) OH MY GOD!!!!! OH MY GOD!!!!! Put the fire out, John!

John and Sonny burst through the kitchen door, John, wearing hot mitts, is carrying a smoldering turkey carcass that has corn popping out of it. He runs to the front door, followed by Sonny with a fire extinguisher. Sean runs out of the kitchen and to the front door, flinging it open. John throws the turkey into the yard as Sonny shoots it with CO2 from the extinguisher. La-Velle comes out of the kitchen, coughing and fanning the smoke away.

LESLIE Sean, what happened?

SEAN (dumbfounded) The turkey exploded!

CHET Exploded?

SEAN All over the kitchen.

LAVELLE And Marie! (beat) Boom, goes the Butterball!

Marie enters, she is spattered with glop, popcorn and soggy bread. She's holding a cookbook.

MARIE (despondent) The kitchen's a disaster. I smell like Aunt Bonnie and my dinner is ruined. I've been planning this meal for months.

(picking at her hair) I don't understand.

(beat)

I followed those damn instructions to the letter!

Popcorn kernels and soggy bread fall out off Marie's hair as she paces around the room.

MARIE (reading) Old fashion Pilgrim stuffing. Two cups of rum and four cups of popcorn kernels.

BONNIE Popcorn? What the hell kind of stuffing is that? Crap Marie, can't you just make stuffing from a box like everyone else?

Marie crosses to Bonnie as John and Sonny come inside. John crosses to Marie and takes the cookbook out of her hands.

MARIE (tense) What the hell do you care Bonnie? You can't eat it anyway; it's not made in a blender. (beat) I followed the damn instructions. Four cups of popcorn and the rest of the stuff!

JOHN (reading) Four teaspoons.

MARIE Huh?

JOHN (sheepishly) It says four teaspoons of popcorn and four cups of bread crumbs.

BONNIE Well, there you are Marie. You might as well crammed a stick of dynamite up its butt!

Marie rips the cookbook from John's hands.

MARIE Let me see that. (reading) Good God. Well, everyone, I guess I really blew it.

BONNIE Or blew it up, in this case.

They try not to laugh as Leslie crosses to Marie.

LESLIE It's okay Mom, there's plenty of other stuff to eat.

MARIE No there isn't! The damn bird exploded all over the yams and the mash potato casserole in the oven. All there is are those nasty dwarf pears, your crappy pie and a bowl of uncooked green beans.

Marie lights a cigarette and holds back tears.

CHET Does that mean Thanksgiving's off? Because I could grab a sandwich at the Hospital.

JOHN NO! (beat) We'll find something to eat.

BONNIE I got a jar of strained lima beans and a bottle of warm strawberry flavored stool softener.

JOHN Hey, there's always that canned ham LaVelle brought.

LAVELLE You know it's not polite to re-gift.

Marie crosses to the phone and dials. She has her back to them.

SONNY How about Chinese?

NURSE They're terrible people.

LAVELLE I'm still down for a duck Dum Dow.

SEAN Sizzling rice soup sounds good.

CHET Kung Pao three of a kind.

SONNY Don't forget the fortune cookies.

LESLIE I got a fortune cookie once that said, "A Merry Heart Doeth Good Like a Medicine." Kind applies to this situation.

BONNIE Never really had a merry heart.

NURSE In Japan there is a saying. 'Warau kado niwa fuku kitaru.'

BONNIE Does it mean, 'Mind your own business?'

NURSE No mean Bonnie. It means, good fortune and happiness will come into the house of those who smile.

LESLIE That's nice. Chet we should try that.

Marie hangs up the phone crossing to Chet with a piece of paper.

MARIE They'll be ready in twenty minutes.

CHET What will?

MARIE Eight hot turkey dinners.

JOHN From where?

MARIE (smiling) Denny's! They never close.

She hands the list to Chet.

CHET Why are you handing me this list?

MARIE Because you're going to go pick them up.

CHET I don't think so. Half time's almost over and I want to watch the game.

Marie and Leslie give him the same "look."

CHET This sucks.

MARIE It's the Denny's on Bel Red Road.

CHET Yeah, I know where it is. That's where I always take Leslie for our anniversary.

LESLIE Nothing says I love you like 'Moons over my Hammy!'

SEAN I'll go with him.

Chet grabs his sweater and stomps out the front door in a huff. Followed by a smiling Sean.

MARIE Okay who wants to help me clean up that disaster in the kitchen?

No one moves as Marie exits into the kitchen.

BONNIE Uh oh, Nurse, ready for round two? Better get a bucket.

Nurse begins to set up the screen.

JOHN I'll get a shovel out of the garage.

SONNY Right behind you.

LAVELLE Do you have any Simple Green?

LESLIE I'll grab a mop.

They exit as Nurse begins her routine. Bonnie moans and winces in pain.

NURSE I told you not to eat prunes on the plane!

MUSIC UP.

"DUBUQUE" by George Winston from the Plains Album.

FADE TO BLACK.

END OF ACT ONE

ACT TWO

MUSIC UP.

"DUBUQUE" by George Winston from the Plains Album.

The lights fade up on the entire cast on stage. Chet sits in the big chair next to the couch where Leslie and Sean sit. Bonnie and Nurse are at their normal spots. John, Marie, Sonny and LaVelle sit at the dining table. They each have a STYROFOAM TAKEOUT CONTAINER from Denny's. On the bar, napkins, little salt and peppers, ketchup packs, mustard packs, extra plastic forks, knives, spoons, etc. In the middle of the dining table sits Bonnie's pears! They silently pick at their Thanksgiving replacement. Nurse spoons a bite of mashed potatoes into Bonnie's mouth.

BONNIE Wipe my mouth, Madame Butterfly.

Nurse wipes her mouth.

NURSE (sotto) Someday after you go, I will sit on a beach and count all the money you generously left me on your death bed.

Nurse smiles and shoves another spoonful of mashed into her mouth.

BONNIE (mouth full of food)Don't count on it.

LESLIE Well, at least there won't be any dishes to do.

JOHN And we managed to salvage Bonnie's dwarves.

MARIE Mine's not bad. How about everyone else?

The polite "mmms" filter through the room.

BONNIE It's CRAP! This isn't turkey. (to Nurse) Hand me a piece.

Nurse hands her a transparent paper-thin piece of turkey. Bonnie whips it out of her hand.

BONNIE Do you call this turkey, Marie? What you destroyed in the kitchen was turkey. This is a sheet of turkey scented Kleenex!

MARIE Give me a break, okay Bonnie?

Bonnie starts to laugh.

BONNIE Two ply turkey!

Bonnie laughs harder. The other's start to laugh. Bonnie holds the piece of turkey to the light as though it's a hundred-dollar bill.

BONNIE This isn't real. It's counterfeit! Counterfeit turkey! That's a federal crime you know? Someone call the FDA.

Bonnie is hysterical. She tosses the turkey to Nurse.

BONNIE Throw this on the wall and see if it sticks! More air, more air!

Nurse turns up the air. Marie slams her silverware on the table. Downing her glass of wine, she pushes the container away from her.

MARIE Forget it!

John tries to save the moment.

JOHN After dinner I'm going to start setting up for the slide show. I've really out did myself this year.

Marie drops her head on the table with a thud!

SONNY LaVelle and I just love your slide show. It reminds me of when we were kids.

BONNIE Slide show? What is it 1950? Nurse, give me a handful of pills. I want to check out right now.

NURSE (smiling) Gladly.

BONNIE I was kidding Kimchee, wipe that smirk off your face. John if you don't mind postponing your trip down memory lane for a bit, I would like to give Sean and Leslie their gifts.

MARIE I need some more wine.

Marie grabs her glass and goes into the kitchen. The phone rings. Sean jumps up and answers it.

SEAN Hello? I know, the battery is dead on my cell phone and I left the charger in my sister's car. (whispering) I can't talk down here. I'll go up to my room, hold on Michael. (setting the phone down) I'm going to take this upstairs. Could someone hang this up after I get it?

Sean bolts upstairs as Marie enters with a black hefty trash bag. She crosses to the phone and listens.

LESLIE Mom, hang up!

Marie scowls at Leslie then slams the phone down.

MARIE Who's finished with their dinner?

BONNIE Oh, dinner? I was trying to figure out what to call it.

MARIE (to Nurse) I think she could fit in this bag. Know what I mean?

Nurse smiles and nods as Marie makes her way around the room dumping trash.

CHET I think I'm going to take a little walk before the fourth quarter starts. Got a little stomach ache.

LAVELLE (smiling) You should see a Gastroenterologist.

CHET Ha, ha!

LESLIE That sounds nice. I'll get my coat.

They both cross to the closet and put on their heavy coats.

SONNY LaVelle, want to join them?

LAVELLE Sure. But wear your muffs. The last thing you need is a cold. You have a voice lesson next week.

Sonny and LaVelle put on their coats too as Marie crosses into the kitchen.

Chet opens the front door.

CHET Hey look, it's snowing.

SONNY I love the snow.

LAVELLE It's so romantic.

They lean their heads together, smiling.

CHET Settle down boys, we're just going on a walk.

They exit outside. John gets up and crosses to the closet.

JOHN Well, I better set up the projector and screen.

BONNIE You're really going to show us those damn slides, huh? I want to give the kids their gifts.

Sean comes downstairs. He seems a little nervous. He crosses to John.

SEAN (hushed) Dad, I need to talk to you and Mom about something. It's kind of a big deal and I don't know how Mom's going to handle it.

JOHN You're not in trouble, are you?

SEAN No, nothing like that. It's a personal thing.

JOHN Oh. (beat) Could you hand me that extension cord?

Sean roots through the closet and gives John the cord.

JOHN Sean, I don't know if today is the right time. Your Mother's been in a mood. The kitchen's still a disaster. Maybe it can wait? (beat) Could you help me set up? I want to be ready for the 'big show' before the other's get back from their walk.

SEAN (defeated) Okay. but I don't think any time will be the right time for Mom.

Sean grabs some folding chairs from the closet and starts to set them up next to a sleeping Bonnie.

Bonnie snores, then wakes.

BONNIE More air Godzilla!

Nurse cranks the valve. Bonnie rustles then goes back to sleep. Sean sets up the chairs in a semi-circle as he watches Bonnie sleep.

SEAN Is she in pain?

NURSE No, but *she is* a pain.

SEAN You know she doesn't mean those ugly things she says to you. She's always been really cool to me and Leslie.

Nurse prepares to give Bonnie her pills.

NURSE I know. I've seen both sides of the coin. Today it's tails. (beat) 'Jinsei ni oite mottomo taisetsu na toki sore wa itsu demo ima desu.'

SEAN What does that mean?

NURSE 'The most important time in life is always the present.' (to Bonnie) Time for your pills.

Sean thinks about what she said as he crosses away to help John.

BONNIE (waking) Do I really need all these pills? You're trying to kill me; I just know it.

NURSE Don't be silly, you're doing fine all on your own.

John crosses in with the projector on a rolling cart as Sean follows with a large screen. John is excited as he sets up the equipment.

BONNIE Good thing I'll be high as a kite in ten minutes.

Bonnie swallows the pills with a gulp. Marie enters with a tray of coffee cups.

MARIE Where is everyone?

SEAN They went out for a walk. (beat) Mom, when you get a chance, I need to talk to you and Dad about something really important. It's kind of serious.

MARIE Serious? You didn't get a girl pregnant, did you?

SEAN (shocked) No!

MARIE STD?

SEAN NO!

MARIE Oh, good. Can't it wait, Sean? Today is already had enough serious.

John crosses to them.

JOHN Well, I'm all set. Now all I need is an audience.

SEAN I really need to talk to you guys.

MARIE My God Sean, what is so important?

SEAN (deep breath) Okay, Mom and Dad...

MARIE (to John) Did you remember to get the Cool Whip?

JOHN Yes, it's in the fridge.

SEAN Really?

JOHN What is it, Sean? You seem really agitated.

SEAN I'm just frustrated.

MARIE (sighing) Me, every day.

JOHN Okay Sean, were all ears.

Sean shifts back and forth.

MARIE Spit it out Sean, we're not getting any younger.

SEAN Okay... (long pause) Do you remember before I started college, you both sat me down and told me what you expected from me? What your goals were for me?

JOHN Yes, that was a very important night.

MARIE I remember, I burnt a roast.

JOHN We laid the ground plans for college.

SEAN Right. (pause) Well, I've made some changes.

JOHN That's exciting. Change can be good.

MARIE It was an expensive roast.

SEAN Uh huh, I hope you think so. (pause) Well, I met this...

The front door swings open with a loud bang! Chet enters followed by the others. He is in the middle of a story.

CHET ...anyway, we ended up removing four feet of his lower intestine and that still didn't fix the problem. Six months and a boat load of bucks, later, he's back in surgery and we're removing another three feet! (laughing) Can you believe it?

SONNY That's a terrible story.

LAVELLE Did he sue you? I would have sued you.

CHET (stops laughing) Why does everybody want to sue Doctors?

It's not an exact science. Not <u>everything</u> is in the text books. We do our best.

LAVELLE Well, it seems your best wasn't good enough.

CHET Jeez, It's just intestines! I thought it was a funny story. We all laughed in the OR!

Sonny takes the coats, and puts them in the closet.

SEAN (frustrated) I give up. You can hear about it from the neighbors.

JOHN What are we going to hear from the neighbors?

MARIE I don't talk to the neighbors.

SEAN (sighs) Whatever.

Sean crosses to the couch and slumps down hard.

JOHN (to Sean) You're here for a whole week, Sean. Whatever it is, it can wait. (excited) Okay everyone get some dwarf pears and coffee... (imitating Ed Sullivan) ...the big shoe's about to begin.

BONNIE Was that supposed to be Ed Sullivan?

John throws Bonnie a 'sorry' look then bounces off to the projector. Chet crosses to the couch.

CHET What's the score? Why is the TV off?

LaVelle and Sonny sit, balancing their dessert plates on their laps. Marie sits next to them.

BONNIE That was the worst Ed Sullivan imitation I've ever heard. I should know, I saw him in person. You obviously NEVER did! He died in 1974, who's your audience any way? (beat) I can't wait for this to be over.

NURSE Life?

JOHN Can somebody please turn out the lights.

NURSE I'm afraid of the dark.

BONNIE You should be!

JOHN Okay, here we go...

MARIE Wait, my wine!?

Marie jumps up, gets her wine, then sits back down.

JOHN Is everyone settled in now? Are we all ready? Nobody needs to do anything else, do they?

BONNIE I do! Now that everyone is in one place, I want to give the kids their presents. (to Marie) And you still haven't opened that damn present I gave you three hours ago.

JOHN (frustrated) That's right Aunt Bonnie. We forgot all about it. Marie why don't you open Bonnie's gift?

John thrusts the gift box towards Marie in frustration.

Marie cautiously takes the wrapped box. she shakes it softly.

MARIE What is it?

BONNIE Really? If I wanted you to know I wouldn't have wrapped the damn thing!

LESLIE You wrapped this yourself? That was very thoughtful.

BONNIE It took me all morning. It tried to get Godzilla to help but she was too busy...

NURSE ...changing your urine-soaked sheets!

SONNY (sotto to Lavelle) Oh, boy. There's a picture…

LAVELLE ...that I'd rather not envision.

LESLIE Mom, just open the gift. Dad, really wants to start the slide show.

Marie sits up in her chair taking a drink of wine. She delicately starts to unwrap the gift.

BONNIE (sarcastic)The suspense is killing me.

NURSE I'll call the coroner.

Marie slowly tears it open. It's the game of 'LIFE'. She stares at, then at Bonnie.

MARIE The game of Life?

BONNIE Thought you might want to play along sometime.

MARIE Really, Bonnie? You shouldn't have.

Bonnie laughs. Marie tosses the game on the floor.

JOHN That was very nice. It's been a while since we've played any games in this house.

CHET You're kidding, right?

SEAN No shit.

JOHN Sean, language?

BONNIE John, give those envelopes to the kids.

JOHN Maybe I should I give them their envelopes after the slide show?

BONNIE NO! I haven't decided whether I'm going to kill myself to get out of watching it yet, so just give them the damn envelopes already.

John crosses and hands the thick envelopes to Sean and Leslie.

BONNIE Sean and Leslie, come over to me please. (to Nurse) Turn down my damn air. I feel like I'm doing a lap in the space shuttle! Maybe they should put the instructions on that tank in Japanese so you can read them.

Nurse adjusts the valve as Leslie and Sean cross to Bonnie. They kneel down next to her.

BONNIE (sincere) Children I want to say how much I have enjoyed watching the two of you grow up and become fine adults. You should be proud of yourselves. There's a lot of temptation and distractions in this world and it's very easy to get knocked off course. You both are doing great, considering your upbringing.

MARIE Bullseye!

Marie rolls her eyes and slugs her wine. Bonnie slowly stands and faces them.

BONNIE (she takes their hands) When I die, ...

NURSE I'll throw a party.

BONNIE ...I want you to remember me not as a woman who had five husbands, or a woman who wished she would've had children, or a woman who was just mean and sick all the time. (her voice trembles) I want you to remember Great Aunt Bonnie as a woman who taught you to always be honest and to hold your heads up high, no matter what. (beat) You both mean the world to me, and what an honor it is to call you family. (sotto) Now, open those damn envelopes before I cry and little Asian Annie over there thinks I have feelings.

Sean and Leslie open their envelopes. As they peer inside, their eyes light up like kids on Christmas morning.

MARIE Well, what is it? My bets on coupons to Baskin Robbin's or the Planetarium.

ALL What is it? Show us. Etc.

SEAN Money.

LESLIE A lot of money.

Chet crosses to Leslie.

CHET How much?

MARIE What?

Sean takes the wad out of the envelope and starts counting.

JOHN Bonnie, I don't know what to say.

BONNIE How about nothing!

LESLIE (stunned) Aunt Bonnie, it's a hundred thousand dollars!

Marie almost falls off her chair.

MARIE (shocked) WHAT? Is there an envelope over there with my name on it?

SEAN Thanks Aunt Bonnie, you're the best.

LESLIE Aunt Bonnie, this is just amazing. (to Chet) Now we can finally get that house we want.

CHET Uh, we'll see.

BONNIE Now, don't blow it! Do something smart with it. (to Leslie) Like keeping it away from your gambling addicted husband.

CHET What the hell, Bonnie?

BONNIE I'm just calling a spade a spade.

NURSE She does too. Usually in public.

BONNIE Shut up Nurse. (to Sean and Leslie) I gave you cash so the damn Government can't get their dirty paws on it. They didn't have to marry a bunch of assholes to build a fortune.

NURSE Sanctity of marriage.

BONNIE (beat) Now, go build your lives, don't waste time and for goodness' sake, be happy!

MARIE (lighting a cigarette) Wonderful, the kids get two hundred thousand dollars and I get the shitty game of 'Life!'

LAVELLE Aunt Bonnie, if I know you were that generous, I would have started dating Sonny a long time ago.

Sonny and LaVelle laugh.

LESLIE (to Chet) You know Chet, I'm thinking about opening up my own bank account.

BONNIE That a girl.

Chet pouts as he crosses back to the couch.

CHET Let's get this stupid slide show over with so I can get out of here. I need my rest. I have a colorectal in the morning.

LAVELLE (sotto to Sonny) And I thought going to the gym in the morning was tough.

Everyone finds their seats as John dims the lights.

JOHN Is everyone settled in? No one needs to do anything? More wine? Bathroom? Walk around the block?

They all stare at him blankly.

JOHN (smiling) Alrighty then, and now without any further ado...

BONNIE Please don't do that stupid Ed Sullivan voice...

JOHN ...I give you a journey down memory lane. (smiling) Happy Thanksgiving everyone.

John flips on the projector. It's white beam of light shoots up and over the audience.

*(*The audience never sees the slides.)*

George Winston's "Corina, Corina" from the Summer album, *begins to play. John clicks on the first slide.*

JOHN There's our house in 1985. (click) There's our house in the winter of 1985. (click) There's our house after we got it painted in 1988. (click) That's the backyard, same year.

MARIE I don't think so, John. I didn't have my garden until the summer of '89. Remember that's the year Leslie split her lip open on that damn swing set Bonnie sent. She had to get eight stitches on her lower lip.

CHET You never told me that.

Leslie shows Chet the small scar on her inside lower lip.

Click!

JOHN Christmas, last year.

SEAN There's Nazi Santa! Wishing you Heil Holidays as you walk by the house.

JOHN (laughing) Sean, be nice.

SONNY John, you always out do yourself with the decorations.

BONNIE Or go overboard.

LAVELLE It's impressive.

NURSE Looks like downtown Osaka.

LESLIE It's beautiful, Dad.

Click!

JOHN Sonny, eleven years old.

SONNY (embarrassed) Oh my Gosh! Where did you find that picture?

They all laugh.

SEAN You look good on the back of a mule, Uncle Sonny.

SONNY (laughing) I'll thank you to keep your opinions to yourself.

LAVELLE I thought you said you were a skinny kid?

They all laugh again. They are having fun.

Click!

JOHN Our children, in the bath tub.

SEAN We're naked!

LESLIE Dad!!! (beat) Look how long my hair was.

CHET You took baths with your brother? (beat) That explains a lot.

Leslie slaps Chet playfully.

SEAN Why did I always have a buzz cut?

MARIE We cut it like that after you got lice.

SONNY Luckily, that was the style.

JOHN I put butch wax on the front to make your hair stand up.

MARIE Sean wanted to look like the Astronauts after he saw The Right Stuff. I love that picture.

Click!

LESLIE That's the summer Aunt Bonnie and Uncle, which one was it?

BONNIE Ken.

LESLIE Yeah, Uncle Ken took us to Disney World. Remember Mom?

MARIE Who could forget the humidity and 110-degree heat.

BONNIE Marie spent most of her time on the Monorail going back and forth to the hotel bar.

JOHN That was a fun summer.

SONNY Didn't you get bit by a spider there too?

JOHN Oh, I'd forgot about that. It was on the Small World ride.

MARIE Jungle Cruise.

JOHN Oh yeah, right.

MARIE You just had to put your hand in that nasty water!

Click!

JOHN Thanksgiving, last year.

LAVELLE Look at me, I had a double chin. And what's with my outfit?

SONNY I tried to donate that sweater to the Goodwill. (beat) They wouldn't take it.

Everyone laughs as Bonnie sits up in her chair.

BONNIE Look, I didn't have an oxygen tank or a Japanese.

CHET (embarrassed) Wow, I'm wearing the same thing.

JOHN Look at all the food on the table.

BONNIE Quite a cry from this year's pitiful bounty.

MARIE And the knife goes in another inch.

She slugs her wine.

Click!

JOHN Group shot from last year.

They all cock their heads to see the slide.

NURSE It's upside down.

JOHN Oops sorry, thought I fixed that. Gremlins in the attic, I suppose.

NURSE Nope, spiders.

BONNIE (tilting her head) Looks better that way.

*John laughs as the music transitions into **George Winston's "The Cradle"** from the Forest album.*

Click!

Everyone stares at the slide.

LESLIE (pause) Who is it, Dad?

SONNY She looks familiar.

BONNIE (happily) It's me! (pause) I remember that vacation. Martha's Vineyard. A long time ago. Look, I'm running on the beach.

JOHN It's a nice picture.

BONNIE (long pause) I'm running. (pause) Thank you, John. I haven't thought about that trip in years. (crying) I was so happy then.

Nurse hands Bonnie a tissue. Bonnie takes the tissue softly, but doesn't let go of Nurse's hand. She brings her hand to her heart and smiles at her.

BONNIE (softly) Thank you for everything.

Nurse smiles at Bonnie. It's a tender moment.

BONNIE But I'll probably be a bitch tomorrow.

Nurse pulls back her hand as John smiles, then 'clicks' on another slide.

LaVelle sits up in his seat. His mouth is a gasp. Sonny smiles as he fondly looks to John.

LAVELLE (long pause) Boom-Pa! (beat) It's me on my Grandpapa's lap. (tearing up) I miss him so much. (beat) Where did you get this?

JOHN Your Mother.

LAVELLE My mother? Oh, John, thank you...you have no idea...

LaVelle begins to sob with his head in his hands. Sonny wraps a loving arm around him smiling.

'Click!'

LESLIE (excited) Oh Daddy, my wedding day. (pause) You remember Chet? (beat) That was the best day.

CHET You looked so beautiful. I was so nervous.

LESLIE You were?

CHET Uh, Yeah... (pause) I couldn't believe someone like you would want to spend the rest of their life with someone like me.

Leslie kisses Chet fondly. John smiles, then looks at Marie. She smiles back.

BONNIE Marie, remember how drunk you got at the reception?

MARIE That's right Bonnie, kill the moment. (beat) Well, at least I didn't make a fool of myself on the dance floor.

BONNIE That's not hard to do when I was laying on it!

They all laugh, even Marie.

Click!

SONNY (surprised) Harold Hill! That's me in Music Man! (to Lavelle) I won an award for that performance. (smiling) Goodness, I haven't thought about that show in years. What a wonderful time we had. Where did you find that picture?

JOHN From the Theater. Stewart Rogers sends his best.

SONNY (emotional) He was our director. I thought he has Alzheimer's?

JOHN He does. But he remembered you right away.

SONNY Really? (beat) Thanks, John.

John smiles at his brother.

Click!

SEAN (agitated) Dad, I thought you promised not to show this picture anymore.

MARIE You look so adorable in your father's uniform.

SEAN I was twelve years old. I look ridiculous.

CHET So naked in the tub you're okay with.

SEAN Shut up, Chet!

JOHN You do not look ridiculous, Sean. I was proud that day when you wanted to become a fire fighter and I'm even prouder now that you're in school actually pursuing it. Son, you come from a long line of firemen. You should be proud.

SEAN I am. It's just... (frustrated) Never mind.

Click!

Marie is startled.

MARIE Turn it off! John, I'm serious! TURN IT OFF!

The MUSIC abruptly stops!

JOHN What's the matter Marie? It's good to remember her.

Marie stares at the picture in silence.

MARIE What's so good about it, John? Look at that picture. Do you see the same thing I do? I don't think so. You couldn't, none of you could. I raised her, I took care of her when she was young, when she was sick... (tearing up) I loved her.

JOHN We all did.

LESLIE She was part of all of us, Mom.

MARIE All I remember is she got hit by a drunk driver and she would have lived if John hadn't told the Vet to put her down. (angry) Now turn the damn slide off!

JOHN I'm sorry, I thought it would be a happy memory for you.

MARIE It isn't! Make it go away.

John turns off the projector.

They all sit in the dark for a moment. John crosses and turns up the lights.

JOHN Well, that's the end.

They all politely applaud, except Marie.

SEAN (abruptly) I'm quitting college!

The applause stops.

JOHN You're what?

MARIE What? Why are you doing that? (beat) Do you know how much money your father and I have spent?

SEAN Yes.

MARIE But you just up and quit. Just like that?

SEAN I've given this a lot of thought.

MARIE Obviously not enough. Did you ever think about consulting us about your decision? Or are we just an ATM now?

JOHN Don't you want to be a Fireman, son?

LESLIE Firefighter, Dad.

MARIE Not now, Leslie.

SEAN No, I want to. I'm just not ready. Do you know what I mean? (beat) I know securing a plan for the future is important. But I've already got one, so I want to explore the world a little while before I commit. Does that make sense?

MARIE Nothing you are saying makes sense.

SEAN My whole life I've done everything you and Mom have wanted.

MARIE Your whole life? You're only 20! What are you going to do? If you think you're going to lounge around this house all day, you'd better think twice.

JOHN Sean, what are you going to do?

SEAN (pause) I'm going to Canada!

Marie screams and drops her wine glass on the floor.

MARIE CANADA? CANADA?! What the hell's in Canada?

CHET I dated a foreign exchange student from Canada. She was hot.

LESLIE Shut up, Chet.

MARIE Yeah Chet, shut up! Canadians hate Americans. Do you know that? It's a country full of draft dodgers, Hockey players and Hookers!

LESLIE Mom, that's silly.

MARIE (to Leslie) Did you know about this?

LESLIE This is not my fault. Sean's an adult now.

MARIE An adult? He doesn't even have the self-discipline to floss! I don't want two college dropouts! (beat) What the hell are you going to do in Canada? Is this about that boy on the phone who keeps calling you?

Marie grabs a new glass of wine as John crosses to Sean.

JOHN (concerned) What's in Canada that's so important?

Sean paces.

LESLIE Tell them, Sean.

SEAN (pause) Have you ever heard of Cirque Du Soleil?

Sonny and LaVelle come to life.

LAVELLE Heard of them?

SONNY They're fabulous. LaVelle and I saw them in Vegas.

BONNIE A very renowned French-Canadian Circus.

Marie spits up her mouth full of wine.

MARIE CIRCUS!! This is about the fucking Circus?

JOHN Marie, calm down. Why don't the three of us talk about this later.

MARIE Everything's always later with you John. I want to talk about it right now.

She pours a glass of wine.

MARIE What the hell are you going to do in the Circus? I know, you can be that clown that has all the dogs that run all over the place knocking him down over and over and over, until it makes you sick. My God John, I our son is running off to join the Circus! The CIRCUS!

Marie starts to laugh hysterically.

SEAN (getting mad) It's not that kind of Circus, Mom.

SONNY Marie, it's fascinating to watch. It's a very talented troupe.

LAVELLE They're worth millions.

NURSE They perform all over the world.

SONNY They're marvelous.

MARIE Marvelous? You know what is marvelous? The mountain of debt his father and I have 'cuz he wanted to go to Berkley!

She takes a big drink of wine.

SEAN Why don't you lay off the wine, Mom! (deep breath) They came to school looking for athletes who were interested in auditioning. Every guy on my team tried out, I got chosen. Out of everyone they chose me. (beat) I'm going to Canada and I'm leaving in the morning. My friend Michael is picking me up. They only choose the best, you should at least be proud of that. But, you won't.

MARIE Michael, the mystery caller?

SEAN Yeah, he was chosen from his school too. But you should know all about it since you were listening on the phone.

MARIE That's a lie.

BONNIE Sean, I'm proud of you. What you're doing takes a lot of guts.

MARIE Bonnie, stay out of this! (to Sean) I don't know who's paying for your little adventure. But from this point on, you're cut off.

Sean waves his envelope from Bonnie.

SEAN I don't need your money.

MARIE How lucky for you! Congratulations Bonnie, you've meddled your way in once again. Why can't you leave this family alone?

JOHN (upset) Marie, stop talking like that. It's Thanksgiving.

MARIE Who cares, John! Go ahead and go Sean. And I want you to know, you don't have my blessing. (beat) Just go! JUST GO!

SEAN (angry) Why can't you be excited that I got this? I get to live in another country, meet new people and be part of something great. (loudly) But you can't see that. Can you, Mom? No, because you're so caught up in what revolves around your tiny little world. At least I'm getting out of this shit hole, and watching you drown your life in alcohol. There're other people in this family besides you. (beat) This is a good opportunity for me. Why can't you see that?

JOHN (rubbing his arm) Please stop it you two. Please!

SEAN (louder) I'm sorry I've fucked up your master plan, Mom.

MARIE You're mean.

SEAN (louder) No Mother, I'm truthful. I know it's hard to hear but, you're an angry alcoholic...and you can shove that blessing up your ass!

Marie slaps Sean hard across the face.

MARIE Go to Canada.

SEAN (shocked) You slapped me!? I can't believe you just hit me. (pause) You want us to be home so bad and when we get here, all you do is push us away. This family sucks.

JOHN (agitated) Sean, stop it! We're a good family. (to the others) We have troubles like everyone else, but we're a good family. A happy family. (beat) Today's just a bad day. We'll be okay. I promise.

John winces as he rubs his left arm and shoulder.

SEAN (agitated) Wake up, Dad. We're not a family anymore. Look at us? It's pathetic. We've grown apart, why can't we just admit that and go on with our lives? Dad, I appreciate what you try to do here. The dinners, the holiday's, the stupid slide shows... (pause) But I'm sorry, it's useless. Just give up and let us hang on to what dignity we have left. (beat) Just give up.

JOHN I'm so sorry, Son. I tried...

John stares at Sean for the longest time. As if in slow motion, the room stands still. John slowly crosses downstage and falls silently to the floor.

LESLIE / SEAN Dad!!??

Marie stands frozen as Chet, Sean, Leslie and Sonny run to John's side.

MARIE (stunned) John? John, honey. What's happening?

SEAN Dad, get up. Chet, help him.

CHET Let me in.

Chet rips open John's shirt throwing his ear to his chest. Nurse crosses in and starts taking his pulse as Bonnie sits in shock.

NURSE His pulse is shallow Doctor. Tachycardic.

CHET Call 911. Someone call 911. We need paramedics. (calmly) Come on, John, don't do this…

LaVelle and Sonny dial their phones.

Marie, Sean and Leslie watch silently in horror as Chet and Nurse perform CPR.

LESLIE (tearing) Daddy please…

SEAN (pause) This is all my fault.

MARIE (pause) No. (crying) It's mine.

Marie slowly puts her arms around Sean and Leslie. They all begin to cry.

George Winston's "LORETTA AND DESIREE'S BOUQUET" Part Two on the Summer album *begins to play.*

SEAN (V.O.) (sadly) I do believe, for that brief moment, we were a family again.

We realized the things we think are important, aren't that important when something really important happens. (pause) Who knows, maybe next year will be different. (beat) And then again, maybe it won't!

Rescue Sirens are heard in the distance as the MUSIC plays.

LIGHTS SLOWLY FADE TO BLACK.

CURTAIN DOWN.

END OF ACT TWO.